SUNBURST CITY
DRAGONS

To request permission, contact the author
at author@sunburstcitydragons.co.uk

ISBN number: ISBN 978-1-8383080-8-7

First edition October 2021
Author: Jane Huddleston
Illustrations and formatting:
David Robinson

www.sunburstcitydragons.co.uk

Look for the  hidden on each page!

JACK'S SECRET

Written by
Jane Huddleston

Illustrated by
David Robinson

Outside Sunburst City, where the hills are wild and green,
Live a group of ten old dragons that most humans haven't seen.
They work and have adventures in a secret world of wonder,
While living in a hidden cave that's halfway up Mount Thunder.
They sneak around so humans don't know where they all have been,
Just two brave children help their dragon friends remain unseen.

Theo's a mechanic
Bob announces for the trains
Lucy is an athlete
Harry unblocks drains
Millie is a writer
Olive farms the land
Alice is a scientist
Jack makes chairs by hand
Yellowbeard's a pirate, now retired with creaking knees
Isla is a bee keeper, she's busy keeping bees.

HARRY

MILLIE

OLIVE

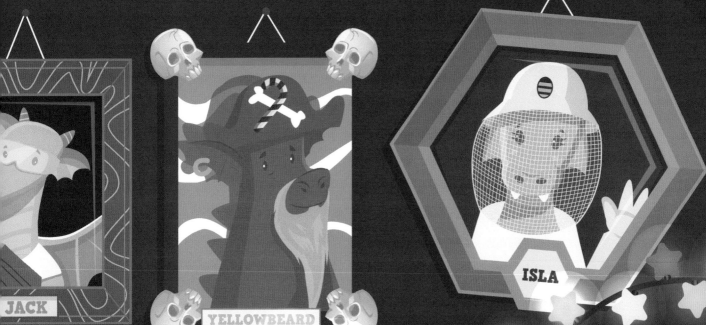

JACK

YELLOWBEARD

ISLA

Jack just loves to make stuff and he's always been so good,
At making gifts and furniture from any kind of wood.
He's even fixed a ship that has been damaged out at sea,
A strong fifteen foot tall, he'll lift a forty foot tall tree.

His dad was great at woodwork, the best joiner in the nation,
He made the British Queen a chair to mark her coronation.
Jack followed this tradition, in his workshop, making chairs,
Occasionally he made a garden bench or spiral stairs.

He's ninety-nine years old with scales that are a sunshine yellow,
Customers don't see him but know he's a lovely fellow.
They email him the measurements and then he works so hard,
Making chairs for people next to Olive's busy yard.

These dragon friends are never seen but certainly are heard,
Being expert on the telephone and at the written word.
On the far side of Mount Thunder a communication mast,
Means their internet connections' always super-duper fast.

One day Jack got an email and he had to read it twice,
'We'd like a chair that's huge, well forty foot to be precise.'
The chair was to be made and then delivered far up North.
'Could it be delivered on December 24th?'

He read the order over, made sure he had understood.
This chair would be so heavy made of strong and solid wood
Jack answered the new customer 'Oh, absolutely, yes!
I'll make and then deliver it, please tell me your address'

The email landed quickly and again he looked aghast,
He grabbed the nearest chair to hand and had to sit down fast!
'The house is at the North pole, it's the big house on the right'
Could this be from Santa Claus? Could Jack find out that night?

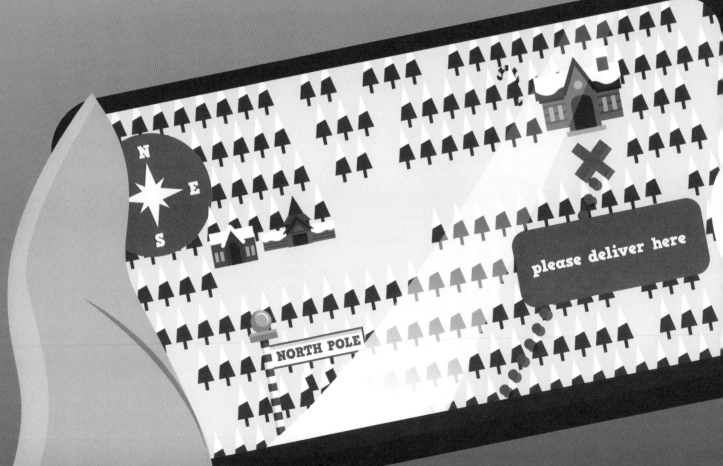

Dragons drop off packages at night all by themselves,
But they've never had to sneak around to hide from clever elves!
Jack could not be spotted, he'd be quiet as a mouse,
Delivering the chair and hiding by the giant house.

The next few weeks were frantic, Jack worked hard to make the chair.
He built the structure strong and then he varnished it with care.
The Sunburst City dragons helped to test this epic build,
So proud their good friend Jack was very kind and super skilled.

Happily Jack emailed 'Your chair's ready to head North!
I'll drop it off outside at night-time on the 24th'
The night had come, Jack grabbed the chair and flapped into the sky,
His friends stood in the yard to wish him luck and wave good bye!

No dragon's ever lifted something this robust and large,
He wished he'd picked a higher number for the postal charge!
It took all of his strength to fly this chair so very far,
Thankfully the way was simple, chase the Northern star.

The snow was falling heavily, a town came into sight.
Jack saw where he should land to end this long and tiring flight.
He slowly and so softly placed the chair down on the ground,
Then snuck behind a snowy tree without making a sound.

It seemed he was so tired he fell asleep and nearly froze,
Then woke up with a jump and sneezed a snowflake off his nose.
He heard a little tinkle from the sky and looked around,
Aghast, he saw a massive dragon land on nearby ground.

Jack yelped in utter shock as he could not believe his eyes,
A sixty foot high dragon had just landed from the skies.
'Ho Ho Ho' a man laughed loudly 'what a brilliant year,
All parcels are delivered and **your** Christmas present's here'

'We're really proud of you my friend, you truly are the best,
To show how much we love you take a seat and have a rest'
The dragon beamed with happiness and sat down in the chair,
'Thankyou Santa Claus, I feel just like a millionaire!!'

'Look' said Santa Claus, 'did you see something by that tree?'
They stared in Jack's direction so he crept out sheepishly,
'I'm sorry' Jack said quietly 'I thought it might be you,
Perhaps if you keep my secret then I can keep yours too!'

'Agreed!' said Santa 'Thank you Jack' he said with gratitude,
'We love the chair, please join us for a hot drink and some food.
We always have a celebration once this night is done,
With all the elves and Mrs Claus, we love our festive fun!'

Jack looked up at the dragon and said 'Why do humans say,
That Santa Claus flies round the world with reindeers and a sleigh?'
The dragon stood up tall and bellowed 'As I am so large,
We draw that on my tummy as a clever camouflage!'

Jack laughed and saw the artwork, these are very clever elves,
They all agreed they'd keep the dragons' secrets to themselves!
Early in the morning they went home in need of sleep
Jack had lots of new friends and a new secret to keep!

Next time you find a present in your house on Christmas day,
Just think maybe a dragon flew it there from far away!
Look all around, check high and low for clues you may have missed,
For if you find a few you may prove dragons do exist.

SPOT THE DIFFERENCE

Can you spot the 5 differences between the 2 pictures? (answers opposite)

ANSWERS

1. Jack's hat has changed colour 2. The 'i' is missing from "Merry Christmas" 3. The DJ Elf's sunglasses are different
4. The big dragon's arm is missing 5. Santa's belt has changed colour